EVERYDAY MINDFULNESS
Exploring Emotions

Published in North America by Free Spirit Publishing Inc., Minneapolis, Minnesota, 2018

Library of Congress Cataloging-in-Publication Data
Names: Christelis, Paul, author. | Paganelli, Elisa, 1985– illustrator.
Title: Exploring emotions : a mindfulness guide to understanding feelings / written by Paul Christelis ; illustrated by Elisa Paganelli.
Description: Minneapolis, Minnesota : Free Spirit Publishing, 2018. | Series: Everyday mindfulness
Identifiers: LCCN 2017060597 | ISBN 9781631983320 (hardcover) | ISBN 1631983326 (hardcover)
Subjects: LCSH: Emotions in children—Juvenile literature. | Emotions—Juvenile literature.
Classification: LCC BF723.E6 C49 2018 | DDC 152.4—dc23 LC record available at https://lccn.loc.gov/2017060597

Reading Level Grade 2; Interest Level Ages 5–9; Fountas & Pinnell Guided Reading Level L

10 9 8 7 6 5 4 3 2
Printed in China
H13770421

Free Spirit Publishing Inc.
6325 Sandburg Road, Suite 100
Minneapolis, MN 55427-3674
(612) 338-2068
help4kids@freespirit.com
freespirit.com

First published in 2018 by Franklin Watts, a division of Hachette Children's Books • London, UK, and Sydney, Australia

Copyright © The Watts Publishing Group, 2018

The rights of Paul Christelis to be identified as the author and Elisa Paganelli as the illustrator of this Work have been asserted in accordance with the Copyright, Designs and Patents Act, 1988.

Managing editor: Victoria Brooker
Creative design: Lisa Peacock

Exploring Emotions

A MINDFULNESS GUIDE TO UNDERSTANDING FEELINGS

Written by
Paul Christelis

Illustrated by
Elisa Paganelli

free spirit
PUBLISHING®

WHAT IS MINDFULNESS?

Mindfulness is a way of paying attention to our present-moment experience with an attitude of kindness and curiosity. Most of the time, our attention is distracted—often by thoughts about the past or future—and this can make us feel jumpy, worried, self-critical, and confused.

By gently moving our focus from our busy minds and into the present moment (for example, by noticing sensations and emotions in our bodies, without judging them or wishing they were different), we begin to let go of distraction and learn to tap into an ever-present supply of well-being and ease that resides in each moment. Mindfulness can also help us improve concentration, calm unpleasant emotions, and even boost our immune systems.

In this book, children are gently guided into mindfulness exercises that encourage an exploration of emotions. By being curious about their "inner weather" and accepting their current emotional experience rather than judging it, they begin to cultivate a healthy relationship with emotions. Instead of identifying themselves with the emotion they are feeling ("I am angry!"), children begin to see that emotions are natural experiences that come and go ("Right now, I am feeling anger in my belly"). The benefits of making this shift are explored in the story.

The book can be read interactively, allowing readers to pause at various points and turn their attention to how they are feeling or what they are noticing. Watch for the 👆▸PAUSE BUTTON in the text. It suggests opportunities to encourage readers to be curious about what's going on for them—in their minds, their bodies, and their breathing. Each time this 👆▸PAUSE BUTTON is used, mindfulness is deepened.

Try not to rush this pause. Really allow enough time for children to tune into their experience. It doesn't matter if what they notice feels pleasant or unpleasant. What's important is to pay attention to it with a friendly attitude. This will introduce them to a way of being in the world that promotes health and happiness.

Everyone notices the **weather** outside, don't they?

Have a look now: Is it sunny or cloudy?
Rainy or dry? Windy or calm? Or something else?

But did you realize that weather also happens inside you?
In fact, if you take a look, you'll feel it right now.
We call this inner weather **emotions**. And just like
the weather outside, emotions are completely natural.

Today is Track and Field Day at school. The weather outside is warm and sunny, but for many children it feels very different. Here's Mateo. He's not feeling warm and sunny at all!

Inside, Mateo is experiencing a different kind of weather. For him, running in a race makes him feel nervous. It's like watching a storm approaching: It can be scary.

And here's Sally, who is also about to run in the race. Her inner weather is different from Mateo's. Can you tell what emotion she's experiencing?

Sally enjoys competing. She's feeling **excitement** and can't wait for the race to start.

◀ 🖱 PAUSE BUTTON ▶

How would you describe Sally's weather? When you are about to run in a race, what's your weather like?

Over at the jump rope race, Manisha has tripped just before the finish line. She's feeling really **angry** with herself. She could have won if she'd been more careful!

How could I be so stupid?

PAUSE BUTTON

Anger can feel like burning hot sun. When you feel angry, where in your body do you feel the burning? Your belly? Your head? Somewhere else?

And this is Caleb. His ankle is broken so he can't participate in any sport today. The sadness and disappointment he feels are like a gray, drizzly day that seems to last forever!

Tom is sitting close to Caleb, but there are no rain clouds over him. He has just completed three events in a row, and now he's feeling **relief** (as well as some achy muscles). For him, relief is like a cool breeze on a hot day.

Later in the day, the weather is changing . . . and guess what?
Just like the weather, the children's emotions are changing, too.

Mateo was nervous, but now he's finished his race and is eating a big bowl of chocolate ice cream.

PAUSE BUTTON

Can you tell what Mateo is feeling now? When you eat something delicious, what feelings do you experience?

Sally's excitement has changed, too. She won her race, but now she's at the hospital visiting her sick grandma. She feels worried and a little sad.

Meanwhile, Manisha is no longer angry with herself. She was awarded a medal for perseverance and now she's feeling proud!

No more drizzle for Caleb! His cast has been removed and now he's feeling happy.

And Tom is back home now with nothing to do.
Relief has turned to boredom.

Changes in our inner weather happen all the time. It's natural and normal. Sometimes the weather feels pleasant—when we feel happy, relieved, or excited, for example. And sometimes it feels unpleasant, like when we feel anger, sadness, or frustration.

The good news is, we don't have to worry about getting stuck with unpleasant emotions, because these won't last forever. Perhaps you are feeling sad this morning, but this afternoon . . . who knows?

We can't predict how we will feel later, and we can't always change our emotions while we are feeling them. But we can learn to be with these emotions as we feel them. We accept them just as they are.

"I know you are here, sadness. It's okay because I know you are just a feeling and you will pass."

"Hello nervous feeling in my belly! You feel uncomfortable but I know you won't stay long."

PAUSE BUTTON

Take a moment to be with what you are feeling right now. How's your inner weather? Sunny? Gloomy? Stormy? Or perhaps there is not a lot going on and you don't feel very much— that's fine too.

"Right now, I'm not feeling anything in particular, and that's perfectly fine."

Sometimes, when weather is very **stormy**, it feels as if you might get blown away by the strong winds. Anger or nervousness can feel like powerful storms!

When you're in a storm of emotions, try naming the emotion you are experiencing. When you name what you are feeling, the storm often calms down a little and doesn't feel so powerful.

"Here's that nervous feeling again."

"This is anger I'm feeling."

So take the time to check your personal weather report every day.

And remember that we all experience many kinds of weather.
Our friends, families, teachers, and pets all have sunny moments,
stormy moments, and not-feeling-very-much-at-all moments.

HELLO,
WEATHER!

HOW ARE YOU
TODAY?

Enjoy the pleasant feelings when they are present,
and remember that the unpleasant ones will pass.

NOTES FOR PARENTS AND TEACHERS

Here are a few mindfulness exercises and suggestions to add to children's Mindfulness Toolkits. These are simple, effective, and fun to do!

Weekly Weather Patterns

Find a place to display a Weekly Weather Chart. This might be on a wall or bulletin board or in children's notebooks or folders. Include days of the week and times of the day. Each morning, ask children to check their inner weather, and then place a colored sticker corresponding to that emotion on the chart. (For example, blue = sad; yellow = happy; red = angry.) Do the same at other times of day. At the end of the week, look at the weather patterns. It's likely that there will be a variety of colors, suggesting changing emotions. If there is a lot of one color, you can talk about this too: Was it a particularly anxious week, or a sad one? Looking at their internal weather this way helps children notice that emotions constantly come and go. This makes difficult emotions easier to acknowledge and accept.

Take Action

Acknowledging difficult emotions can help ease their intensity, but it is also helpful to look at what is needed in that moment to ensure that a child feels safe and resourceful. A cuddle or a hug, perhaps? A few moments alone in a quiet space? Or maybe calling to mind a fond memory or visualizing a special place? The intention of such action is not to avoid the child's feelings. Rather, the action comes from a place of fully accepting the child's experience and compassionately responding to it. This teaches children to self soothe when the going feels rough. Essentially, you are saying, "You feel really sad right now, and that's okay. But you also know that you are safe and loved no matter what you feel."

Magic Minute

Scientific research shows that if we are able to observe the physical sensations of difficult emotions without getting caught up in our thoughts about them, then the chemical component of that emotion flushes itself out of our system, returning us to a state of relative ease. All it takes is a minute or two.

So when a child is in the grip of a strong emotion, suggest taking a Magic Minute to notice it: Where in the body is the angry feeling? What happens when the child pays attention to this feeling? Does it get stronger or softer? Does it move? Are other parts of the body affected? After timing a minute, if the emotion is still intense, take another 30 seconds. The intensity is likely to have waned. A minute often can make all the difference! (It is also possible to take a minute to notice pleasant feelings.)

Invisible Raincoat

Sometimes we can really feel pummeled by stormy emotions. When this happens, it's time to put on your Invisible Raincoat to protect you! If a child needs extra support, invite him or her to imagine a special personal raincoat. What color is it? Does it have an interesting pattern or design? What is it made of? When children are feeling blown away by a rainstorm of emotions, encourage them to slip into their raincoats. This won't stop the storm, but it *can* protect them from getting soaked. Ask them to imagine the raindrops bouncing off the protective layer and to wait patiently for the storm to pass.

Share the Weather

Encourage children to notice and understand that everyone—including parents, other family members, teachers, friends, and pets—experiences changing emotions. We are all in the same boat! Sometimes a parent might be feeling sadness or irritation and may need some space and time to move through it. You can help young people pay attention to this by openly acknowledging and sharing how you are feeling. The intention in sharing feelings is to create an inclusive space where it is possible to bring empathy and compassion to our relationships, without judging one another for feeling the way we do.

BOOKS TO SHARE

Acorns to Great Oaks: Meditations for Children by Marie Delanote, illustrated by Jokanies (Findhorn Press, 2017)

Breathe and Be: A Book of Mindfulness Poems by Kate Coombs, illustrated by Anna Emilia Laitinen (Sounds True, 2017)

Breathe Like a Bear: 30 Mindful Moments for Kids to Feel Calm and Focused Anytime, Anywhere by Kira Willey, illustrated by Anni Betts (Rodale Kids, 2017)

I Am Peace: A Book of Mindfulness by Susan Verde, illustrated by Peter H. Reynolds (Abrams Books for Young Readers, 2017)

Sitting Still Like a Frog: Mindfulness Exercises for Kids (and Their Parents) by Eline Snel (Shambhala Publications, 2013)

Visiting Feelings by Lauren Rubenstein, illustrated by Shelly Hehenberger (Magination Press, 2014)

What Does It Mean to Be Present? by Rana DiOrio, illustrated by Eliza Wheeler (Little Pickle Stories, 2010)

A World of Pausabilities: An Exercise in Mindfulness by Frank J. Sileo, illustrated by Jennifer Zivoin (Magination Press, 2017)